How to Grow a
UNICORN

Rachel Morrisroe · Steven Lenton

PUFFIN

For my brightest lights, Harry and Jack – R.M.

For Paul Booth, whose magic
and sparkle will never fade – S.L.

PUFFIN BOOKS

UK | USA | Canada | Ireland | Australia | India | New Zealand | South Africa
Puffin Books is part of the Penguin Random House group of companies whose
addresses can be found at global.penguinrandomhouse.com.

www.penguin.co.uk   www.puffin.co.uk   www.ladybird.co.uk

 Penguin
Random House
UK

First published 2021
002

Text copyright © Rachel Morrisroe, 2021
Illustrations copyright © Steven Lenton, 2021
The moral right of the author and illustrator has been asserted

Printed in China
ISBN: 978–0–241–39220–1

The authorized representative in the EEA is Penguin Random House Ireland,
Morrison Chambers, 32 Nassau Street, Dublin D02 YH68

A CIP catalogue record for this book is available from the British Library

All correspondence to: Puffin Books, Penguin Random House Children's,
One Embassy Gardens, 8 Viaduct Gardens, London SW11 7BW

 MIX
Paper from
responsible sources
FSC
www.fsc.org   FSC® C018179

Meet Sarah's most marvellous gardening gran –
she's always outside with her watering can.

Digging and planting and sowing and feeding,
pruning and trimming and potting and weeding.

One day, Sarah went to the shops down the street,
in search of a truly spectacular treat . . .

a gift for her gran that was **totally** great.
(It's not every birthday you turn eighty-eight!)

A store caught her eye with some fine golden gilding,
where butterflies bustled and bobbed round the building.

MR POTTIFER'S
PARLOUR OF PLANTS

open

The shop was packed full of unusual flora –
she gasped at the magical vison before her . . .

And there, on the counter, a flytrap was looming,
it spoke with a voice that was
SCARY and
BOOMING.

With a grin so gigantic the plant might just eat her . . .

"WELCOME!"

it said,
as it
swooped down
to greet her.

"Find presents for grandmas
and grandads and aunts,
inside MR POTTIFER'S
PARLOUR OF PLANTS!"

A tiger plant grizzled
and gave her a scare –
a sign on the shelf read:

May bite so **BEWARE!**

The snowdrops
were snow-flaking,
blowing a gale,

while green runner beans
raced about in the hail!

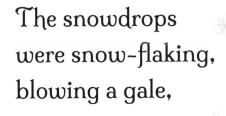

The foxgloves
were boxing,

the cat's paws
were tapping,

the wild bird-of-paradise petals were flapping.

Moo!

A milk-squirting cowslip
was making a racket,

and then Sarah saw
a most wonderful
packet . . .

"My dear," said the flytrap, "these plants can be tricky,
  they won't grow for many – the seeds are quite picky."

But Sarah was thrilled. "It's the greatest gift yet,
  I'll give Gran a grow-your-own unicorn pet!"

At home Sarah followed the planting advice,
she potted with sherbet, then syruped it twice.

"It says to plant one seed – but best to be sure . . ."
She used the whole packet, which held twenty-four!

Later that evening, SS as sleeping . . .

TWENTY-FOUR UNICORN VINES STARTED CREEPING!

By morning, the plants reached as high as the roof.

And then came a whinny, a snort . . .

. . . and a hoof!

Soon, unicorns blossomed from every new flower,
new magical creatures grew hour after hour.

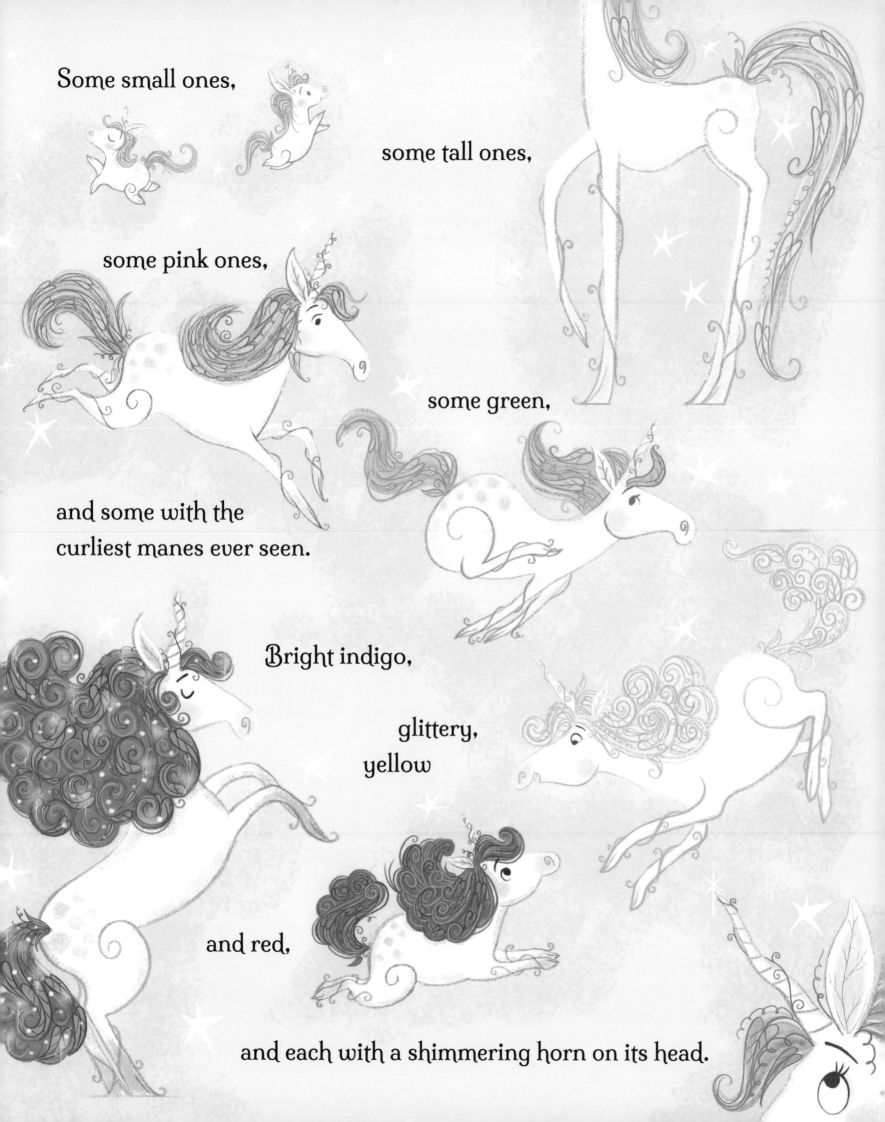

Some small ones,

some tall ones,

some pink ones,

some green,

and some with the
curliest manes ever seen.

Bright indigo,

glittery,
yellow

and red,

and each with a shimmering horn on its head.

"I've planted too many!" cried Sarah with shock,
at the sight of the unicorns running amok.
Now, freshly grown unicorns don't take instruction –
it turns out they're brilliant at PARTY DESTRUCTION!

They nibbled Gran's dress and then ate all the cake.
The half-eaten party food lay in their wake.

They burst the balloons with the horns on their heads,

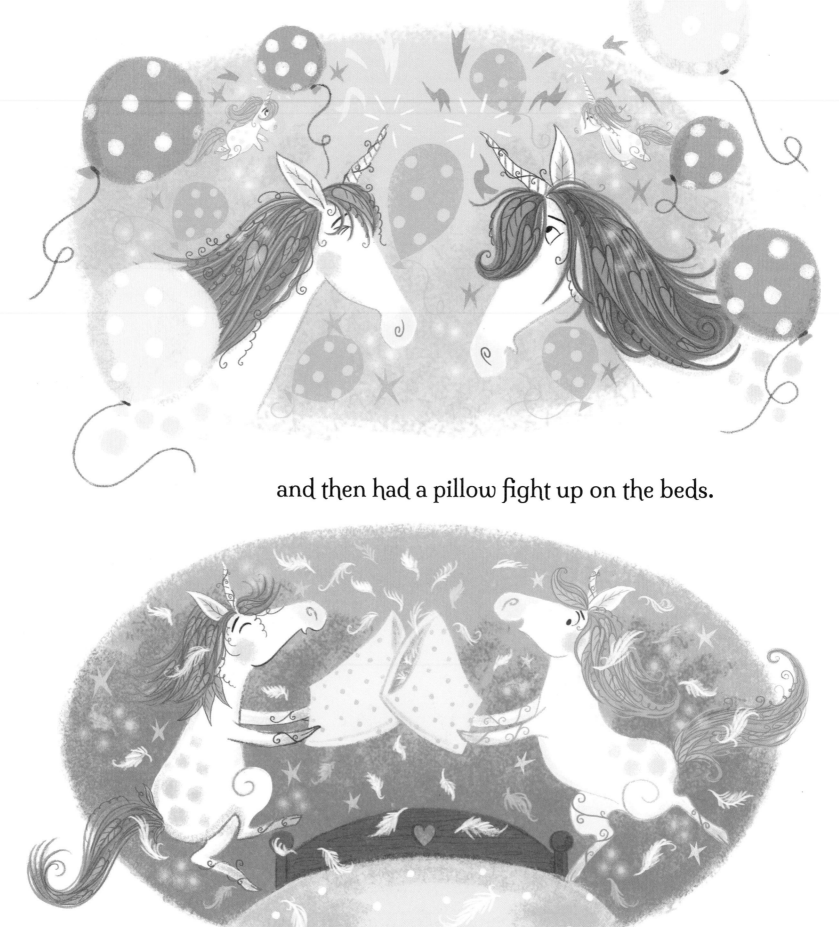

and then had a pillow fight up on the beds.

"I'm sorry," said Sarah. She hung her head sadly.
"Your birthday is going so terribly badly."

Gran smiled, though her party was torn up in tatters.
"Your gift was so thoughtful and that's all that matters.
We can't keep them all though, the cottage would pop –
they'll have to go back to the gardening shop!"

So, to Mr Pottifer's Parlour they hurried,
but Sarah was sad
and incredibly worried . . .

"I'm scared Mr Pottifer's going to be cranky!"
Her gran dried her tears on a polka-dot hanky.

They soon reached the parlour, the bell gave a tinkle,

as unicorns squeezed in the shop, all a-twinkle.

She told Mr Pottifer what had gone wrong . . .

And that's when a unicorn's bum made a pong!

It blushed as it pooped and they all held their noses.
The magical plop fell on top of the roses.

They looked on with shock as in front of their eyes,

the bush shook
and shuddered . . .

and tripled in size!

Sarah then had the most brilliant idea:
"People can have perfect gardens all year!"

She painted some posters and stuck them on railings,
     then folded up fliers and sent them in mailings,

UNICORN HELPERS:
RESULTS GUARANTEED!

No need for gadgets
to mow, trim and weed!

For gardens more gorgeous
than ever before,

fresh unicorn poop
makes the purest manure!

But what of Gran's birthday?
    She got the best present –
    her garden wins prizes for being so pleasant!

And Sarah now helps in the magical store,
to grow most extraordinary creatures galore.

A new seed she's planted
has just started glowing . . .

For dragodils often breathe fire
as they're growing!